MEET ALL THESE FRIENDS IN BUZZ BOOKS:

Thomas the Tank Engine
Fireman Sam
The Animals of Farthing Wood
Skeleton Warriors
Puppy In My Pocket
Kitty In My Pocket
Pony In My Pocket

First published in Great Britain in 1996 by Buzz Books
an imprint of Reed Children's Books
Michelin House, 81 Fulham Road, London SW3 6RB
and Auckland, Melbourne, Singapore and Toronto.

Based on a Martin Gates Production

ISBN 1 85591 552 9

Printed in Italy

Welcome to the Willows

Story by Katie Vandyck

from the animated series

It was the first day of spring. Mole woke, sniffed the air and yawned.

"I do believe . . . Yes! Spring at last! And that means spring cleaning!"

He leapt out of bed, gathered his brooms, brushes and dusters and got to work. After a short while he stopped.

"Bother," he said crossly, as he looked at the mess.

He grabbed his coat and disappeared out of the door. He skipped across the fields, chatting merrily to the creatures that he met.

After some time he came to a hedge, scrambled through, and there before him lay . . . the river. Mole couldn't believe his eyes.

"Oh my!" he gasped. He sat with his legs in the water and gazed and gazed at the wonderful sight of the beautiful river.

Rat was watching Mole from his deck chair on the other side of the river.

"Hello, Mole," he said, his eyes twinkling

with amusement. "Would you like to come over?"

"Oh yes – but how?" asked Mole.

Rat leapt into his rowing boat, untied it from its moorings and sped across the river to Mole. Rat was amazed that Mole had never been on a boat before.

"Believe me, my young friend," he said, "there is nothing – absolutely nothing – half so much worth doing as simply messing about in boats." He added, "If you've really nothing else on hand this morning, supposing we drop down the river together, and have a long day of it?"

Mole was delighted.

"Let's start at once!"

Rat hurried back to his house, brought back a bulging picnic hamper and off they went. After a while they reached a little backwater surrounded by peaceful meadows.

"Oh my, oh my, oh my," whispered Mole as he stared entranced at the view. Rat found a spot for their picnic and the two of them feasted on cold chicken, cold tongue, cold ham, pickled gherkins, ginger beer and lemonade. Just as they were finishing the last crumbs, Otter appeared at the water's edge.

“Greedy so and so’s,” he joked, “why didn’t you invite me?” He shook hands with Mole and sat down beside them.

"Tell us who's out on the river?" asked Rat.

"Toad's out for one," said Otter.

Toad was well-known for his whims and the friends weren't surprised to hear about his latest craze for rowing boats.

Rat laughed. "It's always the same, whatever he takes up, he gets tired of it, and then he starts on something fresh."

As he spoke, Toad whizzed past in his boat, waving to the three on the bank, almost losing an oar as he shot by. He disappeared from view to the sound of frantic splashing and angry quacking.

"Oh dear, time to lend assistance, I think," sighed Otter and slid off in a trail of bubbles to help his friend.

Rat stood up.

"Well, well, I suppose we ought to be moving."

"Ratty," asked Mole, "may I row the boat?"

Rat said that Mole ought to take a few lessons before rowing on his own. Mole hung his head in disappointment. Then, without quite knowing why, Mole suddenly leant forward and grabbed the oars. Rat was knocked head over heels into the bottom of the boat.

"Stop it, Mole!" shouted Ratty, his feet waving in the air. "You can't do it; you'll have us over!"

Mole stumbled into Rat's seat and somehow managed to keep hold of the oars. When he tried to row, however, he missed the water and the oars flew out of his grasp. He lost his balance, fell backwards and landed heavily on top of Rat.

"Aargh!" shrieked Mole.

"Ow!" shouted Rat as the boat began to rock dangerously.

Mole tried to get to his feet but the boat tipped over and flung them both into the river with a loud 'splash!'

"Help!" spluttered Mole, flailing hopelessly around in the water.

Rat grabbed him by the back of the neck and hauled him to the safety of the shore. There he stood wet and bedraggled and very ashamed of himself.

Rat rubbed him up and down on the back until he had caught his breath and then plunged back into the river to retrieve the hamper.

Mole tried to apologise but Rat, cheerful as ever, wouldn't let him.

"That's all right, bless you!" he laughed. "What's a little wet to a water rat. Don't think any more about it."

Rat suggested that Mole should stay with him and learn how to swim and row properly. Mole couldn't believe his luck. He stammered out his thanks. They dried themselves off and settled down in Rat's cosy parlour to plates piled high with toast, crumpets and cake. Rat told Mole all about life on the river until Mole's head began to nod and before long he was asleep.

Spring turned into summer and Rat taught Mole a great deal about the arts of the river. Mole became quite good at swimming and rowing and would often take the oars when they went on their picnic trips.

One morning Mole asked Rat, "Won't you take me to call on Mr Toad? I've heard so much about him, and I do so want to make his acquaintance."

Rat readily agreed and they paddled upstream to where Toad lived. Toad Hall was a big manor house. Rat pointed out the stables and the grand banqueting hall. At the bottom of the lawn stood a boat house where a barely-used boat stood idle.

"I see," said Rat. "Boating is played out. I wonder what new fad he has taken up now."

They came upon Toad, sitting in a wicker chair, battling with a large map.

"Hooray – this is splendid," he cried. "I was just going to send a boat down for you, Ratty. I want you badly – both of you." He smiled at Mole.

He took them to the stable yard and pointed to a brand new Gypsy Caravan.

"There you are!" he cried. "There's real life for you. The open road. Travel, change, interest, excitement! Come inside and look at the arrangements."

Inside the caravan lay every single thing you might need for an adventure, including bacon, jam, dominoes and a birdcage. Much against Rat's better judgement, Toad persuaded them to come along with him. They were to start at once.

At first Toad enjoyed himself very much. It was a perfect day to stroll along and Toad shouted hearty greetings to every animal he met.

One rabbit remarked, “That’s a very fine cart you have there, Sir.”

“Indeed it is;” Toad replied proudly, “most expensive one on the market!”

Mole was very happy to be part of such an adventure and even Rat kept quiet though he would rather have been back on the river. That night they cooked and ate by the camp-fire. Toad went to bed and left Rat and Mole to take care of all the chores. They were rather cross about this so the next day they made sure Toad did more than his share of the work.

Toad was just beginning to think to himself that a little domestic help might make life on the road more fun when he heard a faint "Poop Poop" in the distance. The animals turned round and saw a small cloud of dust appear behind them on the road. It seemed to be getting nearer and nearer and bigger and bigger. Suddenly, out of the cloud, a car came speeding towards them. The horse reared up in terror and the caravan rolled backwards into the ditch! Rat and Mole shouted angrily after the disappearing car but Toad sat stock still in the road. He was bewitched.

"Poop Poop!" he uttered faintly.

The innkeeper from a nearby village helped Rat and Mole recover the caravan from the ditch, though Toad was no help at all.

He sat on a bench outside the inn, looking vacant and whispering, "Poop Poop!"

Rat took charge and together he and Mole pushed Toad on to a home-bound train and the three of them returned to Toad Hall. They held a dazed Toad up by the arms as they wound their way up the driveway to the Hall. They left him there, still murmuring, "Poop Poop!"

"Heard the news?" Rat asked Mole the next day. "Toad went up to town this morning, and he has ordered a large and very expensive motor-car . . ."